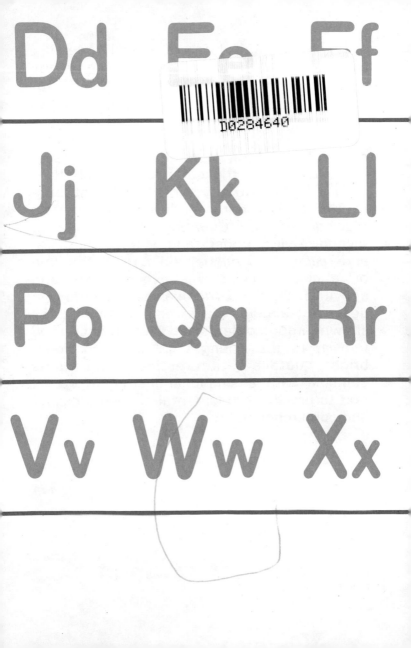

The quality and depth of a child's memory and observation can be surprising, and many authorities maintain that the best time for learning is when everything is new and therefore important and memorable to the child.

The Ladybird Early Learning series includes six books designed to help parents amuse, interest, and at the same time teach their child. *Shapes, Colors,* and *abc* all contribute to the child's early understanding of the reading process. *Counting* teaches him to recognize and understand simple numbers, and *Telling the Time* helps him relate the time on a clock face to his everyday life and activities. *Big and Little* deals with words that describe relative sizes and positions, all shown through objects and scenes that will be familiar to the young child. In each book, bright, detailed, interesting illustrations combine with a simple and straightforward text to present fundamental concepts clearly and comprehensibly.

LADYBIRD BOOKS, INC.
Lewiston, Maine 04240 U.S.A.
© LADYBIRD BOOKS LTD MCMLXXVIII
Loughborough, Leicestershire, England

Printed in England

abc

illustrated by GERALD WITCOMB

Ladybird Books

apple

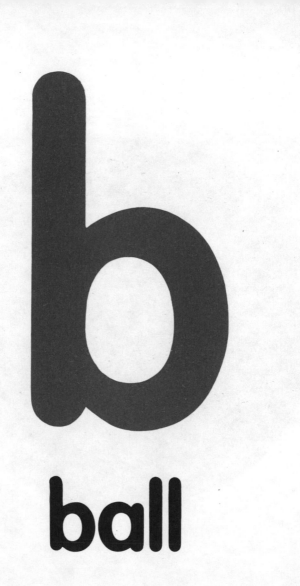

ball

C

cat

duck

e

elephant

fish

g

goat

h

hammer

insect

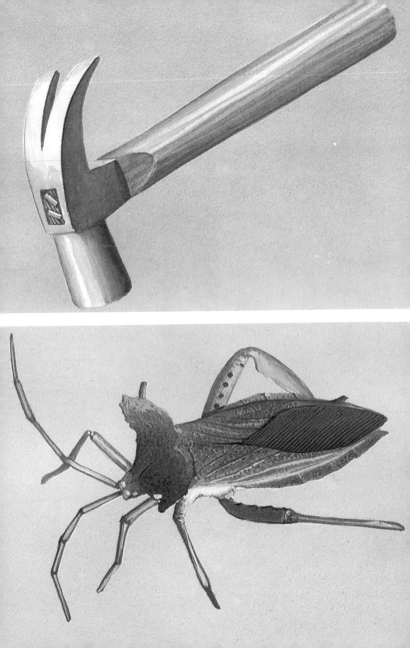

jar

kite

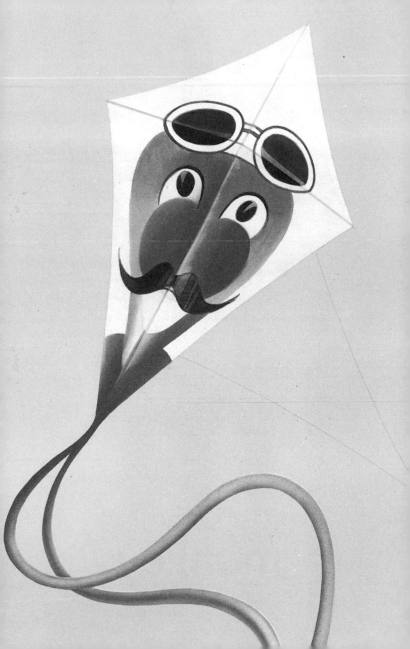

l

ladder

monkey

newspaper

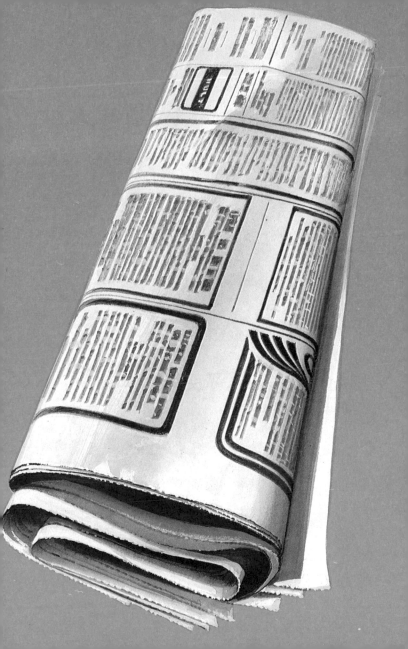

O

ostrich

pencil

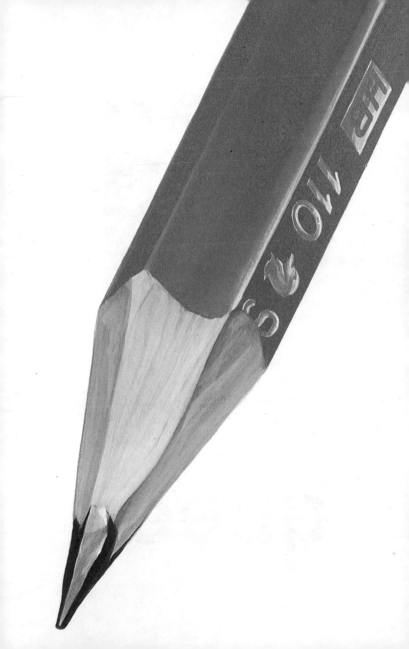

q

queen

ring

S

sun

teeth

umbrella

volcano

watch

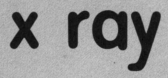

x

x ray

x as in box

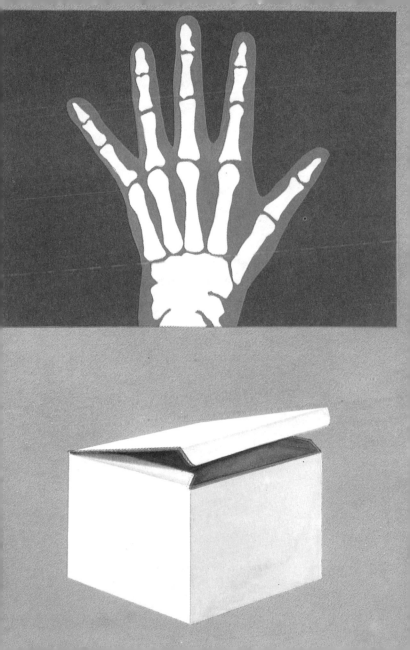

yacht

zebra